Waltham Forest Libraries

ß

Please return this item by the last date ~~~~~~~~~~~~~ may be
renewed unl~~~

Jan. 18

ID626621

Sweet Cherry
Publishing

Published by Sweet Cherry Publishing Limited
Unit 36, Vulcan House
Vulcan Road
Leicester, LE5 3EF
United Kingdom

First published in the UK in 2017
ISBN: 978-1-78226-256-5
©Stephanie Baudet 2015
Illustrations ©Creative Books
Illustrated by Joyson Loitongbam

Mr Pattacake goes to Buckingham Palace

Wai Man Book Binding (China) Ltd. Kowloon, H.K.

Pattacake, Pattacake, baker's man,
Bake me a cake as fast as you can;
Pat it and prick it and mark it with P,
Put it in the oven for you and for me.

Pattacake, Pattacake, baker's man,
Bake me a cake as fast as you can;
Roll it up, roll it up;
And throw it in a pan!

Pattacake, Pattacake, baker's man.

MR PATTACAKE
goes to
BUCKINGHAM PALACE

One morning, something very unusual happened. Mr Pattacake received not just one letter in the post, but *two*.

Two letters was certainly a good enough reason for Mr Pattacake to do his silly dance – all the way from the hall and into the kitchen, where his ginger cat, Treacle, was nibbling contentedly on his breakfast.

The house almost shook as Mr Pattacake hoppety-hopped his way through the door, waving a letter in each hand. His big chef's hat wobbled so violently that it almost fell off his head.

This was so unusual that Treacle actually paused whilst eating, just to look up and see what all the excitement was about.

'My talent for cooking has been recognised at last,' said Mr Pattacake, not very modestly. 'I am going to be awarded a CPE by the Queen herself!'

Treacle did not know what a CPE was, so he was not impressed. Mr Pattacake would have to explain what it meant first to get any sort of reaction out of him. Mr Pattacake could always read what Treacle was thinking; he had been around cats all his life.

'A *Chef Par Excellence*,' he said, which still didn't mean a lot to Treacle, since he didn't speak French... or any other language, for that matter.

'It means an award for being a great chef,' said Mr Pattacake, patiently. 'I have to go to Buckingham Palace next week to receive it. But... I'm afraid the letter says: *Please do not bring your cat because he might upset the corgis.*'

Treacle's ears flattened in dismay. He couldn't go because of the corgis! Why did he have to miss out because of them? Couldn't they be shut in a room, or something?

'No,' said Mr Pattacake, reading the cat's mind again. 'You *cannot* shut the royal corgis in a room just so you can come with me. I'm afraid you will have to miss out on this one, Treacle. However...'

That had been the letter in his right hand. Now Mr Pattacake waved the letter in his left hand, indicating that all was not lost.

'We have a job to do on that same morning, which will fit in nicely with the visit. I'm not due at Buckingham Palace until four o'clock so we can do this job first and still have plenty of time. We've been asked to provide picnic hampers for a family who are going on a hot air balloon flight. It's the lady's birthday and it will be her, her husband and their two children.'

Treacle had seen hot air balloons before, floating past on still days, but he had no wish to fly in one.

'No, we shan't be going on the flight,' said Mr Pattacake, shaking his head. 'But we will get the chance to see the balloon being inflated and taking off. They are enormous, and very colourful, too.'

Treacle couldn't get too excited about this, he was still put out by the fact that he wasn't allowed to go to Buckingham Palace. Not only that, but Mr

Pattacake always said he was his assistant. Once he had even said, 'Where I go, Treacle goes.'

Mr Pattacake was nodding. 'I can't argue with the Queen, though, can I, Treacle?'

Treacle lay down with his head on his paws, looking miserable, while Mr Pattacake sat down at the table with his pen and paper. He needed to make a list of what he would need for the picnic. Mr Pattacake always began by making a list, and he was sure that it was one of the secrets to his success.

When he had finished the list, he read it out to Treacle, who was still sulking.

All sorts of delicious things were on it, like:

Scotch eggs,

sausage rolls,

cheese straws,

asparagus and cheese tart,

salad and crusty bread...

and lots more.

There would also be champagne for the adults and fizzy pop for the children.

Treacle looked hard at Mr Pattacake. He had forgotten the main dish (in Treacle's opinion).

'Chocolate mice!' said Mr Pattacake, suddenly remembering. 'Of course!'

Chocolate mice were Mr Pattacake's specialty and Treacle always ate the scraps, even though chocolate isn't good for cats.

On the day before the **BIG DAY**, Mr Pattacake went off in his little yellow van to get all the ingredients for the picnic hampers he was going to put together.

Then he prepared the food. It took a long time, and there was the usual disaster with the chocolate mice, but at last it was all prepared and ready for an early start the next day.

It was a perfect day for a balloon ride. Clear skies and no wind.

Mr Pattacake loaded the four hampers into the little yellow van and then he and Treacle set off for the launch site.

When they arrived at the field, the balloon came into sight, already half inflated. It had red, white and blue stripes. It looked magnificent! They both gazed up at its enormous sides with awe. Under it, on the ground, sat the big basket that would carry the people up into the air. It was attached to the balloon by ropes, and one long rope in particular was anchoring the balloon to the ground so that it didn't drift away.

There was a big roaring noise, which Mr Pattacake knew was the burner blowing hot air into the balloon. Treacle flattened his ears. He didn't like the sound one bit.

'Over here, Mr Pattacake,' said one of the men, who was standing near the balloon basket. 'Please put one hamper into each corner so that the weight is balanced. Will you be able to manage?'

'Yes, thank you,' said Mr Pattacake. They wouldn't be going for a ride in it, but it *would* be good to stand in the basket with that huge balloon above them. He opened the doors of the van and lifted out the hampers, putting them on the ground beside the basket.

Two children ran up to him.

'Hello, are you Mr Pattacake, the man who has made all our picnic food?' asked the little boy. His name was Oliver.

Mr Pattacake nodded and smiled brightly at him, looking up. Next to the boy was a girl who looked a bit older than him. 'Hello, are you going up in the balloon, too?'

The girl nodded enthusiastically. 'It's our Mum's birthday treat. We're all going. My name is Sally,' she said. Then she saw Treacle. 'Is this your cat?' She bent to stroke Treacle, who closed his eyes and purred loudly as he rubbed against her legs.

'That's Treacle,' said Mr Pattacake. 'Well, I hope you all have a lovely time in the balloon and I also hope you enjoy the picnic.'

The two children said goodbye and ran off. They were so excited that they could barely keep still.

'Let me give you a hand,' said the balloon man, walking over to them. 'I don't think your cat is going to be much help.'

Treacle glared at the man. He didn't like what he had just heard. *Of course* he was a help. He couldn't lift the hampers, but Mr Pattacake couldn't do without him. He was very good at clearing up the food which dropped on the floor.

'You get in the basket, Mr Pattacake,' said the man, 'and I'll lift the hampers in.'

Mr Pattacake lifted his leg over the side of the basket with great difficulty. It was quite high. Treacle, on the other hand, jumped up effortlessly. It was easy for a cat.

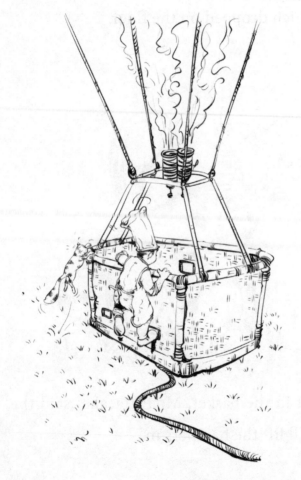

Mr Pattacake put each of the four hampers into each of the four corners, just as the man had asked. The balloon was now fully inflated and was drifting above them in the breeze, pulling at the rope that was holding it to the ground.

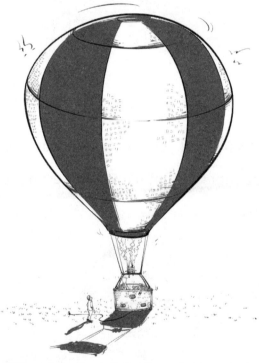

'Come on, Treacle, our job is done here. Let's go home and get ready to go to Buckingham Palace.'

Treacle was still grumpy after what the man had said, but *now* his scowl was even worse as he remembered that *he* was not going to Buckingham Palace.

Mr Pattacake was just about to climb out of the basket, when it **juddered** slightly.

And then it lifted off the ground altogether.

OH NO!

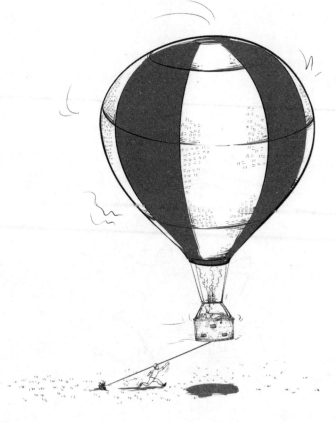

Alarmed, Mr Pattacake stood up and looked over the side. The balloon was already rising higher and higher in the air.

It had taken everyone by surprise and, despite people running to grab the tethering rope in time, it was now too high to reach.

Where it had been anchored to the ground, Mr Pattacake could just make out a small dark shape, its little face and pricked up ears watching their ascent.

It was that mischievous tortoiseshell cat, Naughty Tortie!

'**Oh DRIBBLE!**' exclaimed Mr Pattacake. 'Naughty Tortie has bitten through the tethering rope! *Now* what shall we do? I don't know how to fly a balloon.'

Mr Pattacake was so nervous that his big chef's hat wobbled.

It wobbled so much that it fell right off his head and sailed over the edge of the basket. He watched it drift down, and billow out like a strange parachute, until it was just a small white dot.

Treacle couldn't see anything from where he was at the bottom of the basket, and he was not about to jump onto the side. All he could see was the big red, white and blue balloon above them, free at last, sailing higher and higher.

The man was shouting something and waving, but Mr Pattacake couldn't hear. All they could do, he supposed, was wait until the hot air in the balloon cooled down, making it float back down to earth.

When, and where that would be, he didn't know.

It was so quiet and peaceful. The only sounds they could hear were the occasional car engine and the squeal of children's laughter as they played. Over the green fields and woods they went. Over villages and cornfields and rivers they soared.

Mr Pattacake managed to make a harness from some of the ropes, so that Treacle could sit on the side and enjoy the scenery, too, with no danger of falling out.

Suddenly, Mr Pattacake remembered something. '**Oh DRIBBLE!** What about my award at Buckingham Palace? I'll be too late.'

Treacle didn't like to be unkind, but he couldn't help but smile his cat's smile to himself. At least he wouldn't be the only one missing out now.

Soon there were more and more houses down below them, and bigger and bigger towns. Then they came to a big river.

The balloon was getting lower as the air inside of it began to cool, and Mr Pattacake didn't know how to turn on the burners to blow in more hot air. They were going to land soon, whether they liked it or not.

They could hear the noise of the traffic, and
they could see the people looking up at them.

There were lots of spires and steeples and other tall buildings. There was a big wheel as well.

Mr Pattacake gasped. 'We're in London,' he exclaimed. 'There's the London Eye and there's the Shard. Look, Treacle, that tall, pointed glass building.'

Treacle *was* looking, his eyes wide with fear. Even he knew that pointy glass things and balloons didn't go well together. He had seen enough balloons at birthday parties to know what happened if pointy things were stuck into balloons.

BANG!

But luckily, they drifted past.

Mr Pattacake was quiet, watching as they went lower and lower, getting nearer and nearer to the tops of the buildings. Landing a balloon in the middle of London was not a good idea at all.

They were really low now.

'Hang on tight for landing,' said Mr Pattacake in a shaky voice, bracing himself.

Treacle flexed his claws, ready to dig them into the wicker of the basket.

They could see an open green area with a lake in the middle. On the vast lawn there were big tents and lots of people, all gazing upwards in awe.

As the realisation dawned, Mr Pattacake looked at Treacle excitedly. 'I can't believe it! It looks very much like…'

BUMP!

'Buck-aaaaaa-ouch!' The basket hit the ground just as Mr Pattacake attempted to tell a very confused Treacle where they were.

It tipped over on its side, almost spilling them both out onto the grass. Then the big balloon dragged the basket across the lawn, heading straight for the lake. They may have ended up right in it if some men hadn't grabbed the ropes and dragged the balloon down, pushing all the air out of it. Finally it lay in a red, white and blue heap of material on the green grass.

Treacle jumped out onto the lawn and quickly composed himself, pretending to wash his paw, although everyone knows that a cat sometimes does that when it's embarrassed. What an undignified landing in front of *all* those people!

Mr Pattacake, on the other hand, had an even more embarrassing tumble, because he wasn't quite as nimble as Treacle and took longer to get to his feet. In fact, he needed some extra help.

'Now, sir. Who are you?' asked one of the men in uniform who had deflated the balloon and helped Mr Pattacake up. 'Do you realise where you've landed?'

'Yes,' said Mr Pattacake, a little out of breath as he dusted himself off. 'It's Buckingham Palace.'

'It is, indeed,' said the man, sternly. 'And we are the security men guarding the Queen, and must ask you to come with us for questioning.' Two of the security men each took one of Mr Pattacake's arms and marched him away, while all the garden party guests looked on curiously.

No one seemed to be that bothered about Treacle, which both pleased and annoyed him. He did *not* want to be taken away to be questioned, yet he *did* think he was important enough to be *noticed*.

Meanwhile, Mr Pattacake was taken into a room and asked to sit down.

'Why did you land here?' asked one of the men, glaring at him. 'This is a severe breach of security.'

'I didn't mean to,' said Mr Pattacake, his voice shaking slightly under the security men's hard stares. 'I'm a chef and I'd made some picnic hampers for a lady who was *supposed* to go on a balloon flight with her family. But as I was loading the hampers onto the basket, someone (he didn't think it was worth naming the culprit) untied the rope and we took off. I can't fly a balloon so I just had to wait until it landed.'

The security men did not look as though they believed him. But Mr Pattacake had an idea. He reached into his pocket and took out the invitation he had received from the Queen.

'By coincidence,' he said, proudly, 'I am to be awarded a CPE by Her Majesty this afternoon at four o'clock.'

The security man looked at the invitation closely, as if suspecting that it might be fake.

'Can you prove you are who you say you are?' he asked.

'Well,' said Mr Pattacake. 'I do have my chef's apron on and I *was* wearing my big chef's hat, but it blew away when we were in the balloon.'

'We?' said the security man, looking around the room.

'Me and my cat, Treacle,' said Mr Pattacake. 'He would vouch for me – if he could talk.'

'We cannot take a cat's word as proof,' said the security man.

'Ah! I have it!' said Mr Pattacake. 'If you look in the basket you will see the four hampers of food I made. Why else would I have been in the basket?'

That seemed to satisfy the security man. He went off at once, leaving Mr Pattacake with the second man, who said nothing at all.

It was about ten minutes before the first man came back.

'I checked the food and I also spoke to Her Majesty,' he said. 'You are, indeed, going to receive an award, in fact, you can go straight in now. I'll show you the way, sir.'

Mr Pattacake followed the security man through a maze of corridors, and he wondered what Treacle was doing; he hoped he wasn't getting into any trouble.

At last they reached the grand ballroom, where the ceremony was being held. Mr Pattacake gasped in awe as they entered the enormous room, with its red carpet, crystal chandeliers and ornate gold decoration. He stood in line with all the other people who were receiving awards as well.

The Queen herself stood on a platform guarded by a line of five Yeomen of the Guard in their red and gold uniforms and black hats. On her right stood the Lord Chamberlain, stating each person's name as they stepped forward to receive their award.

At last, it was Mr Pattacake's turn.

'Mr Percy Pattacake, *chef par excellence*,' announced the Lord Chamberlain.

Mr Pattacake stepped up to the Queen. She bent and pinned the medal to his chest, smiling as she congratulated him warmly. He felt so proud. Then, just as he was about to step back, the Queen leant forward to say something to him.

'I understand that you brought your cat after all, Mr Pattacake,' she said in a whisper. 'I do hope he doesn't upset the corgis.'

'I'm extremely sorry, Your Majesty,' said Mr Pattacake, embarrassed at having disobeyed the Queen. Would she have him thrown into the Tower? 'I didn't expect to arrive by balloon.'

The Queen frowned slightly. 'What on earth were you doing in a balloon?'

'I had prepared some picnic hampers for someone's birthday,' he said, sadly. 'But as I was loading them into the basket someone untied the tethering rope.'

'Picnic hampers?' The Queen smiled broadly. 'Did you say picnic hampers, Mr Pattacake?'

'Yes, Ma'am.'

'I think you have just saved the day,' said the Queen. 'One of my chefs has gone off sick and there isn't enough food for the garden party. Could we use your picnic food?'

'Yes, of course, Ma'am. It would be an honour to help you.'

The Queen waved a hand at two footmen. 'Please help Mr Pattacake to unload the picnic hampers from the balloon basket and put the food on the tables,' she said.

The footmen bowed stiffly.

'Well done, Mr Pattacake.' The Queen smiled, and Mr Pattacake took several steps backwards, as you had to do when leaving the Queen, and then followed the footmen out into the grounds to where the basket still lay on its side.

He looked around.

There was *still* no sign of Treacle. Mr Pattacake's heart sank.

They reached the basket and the footmen unloaded the hampers and carried them to the tables in the marquees.

Mr Pattacake's thoughts were suddenly interrupted by a commotion. There was a lot of yapping and three angry corgis streaked past, chasing a terrified Treacle, who dived into one of the marquees, leapt onto a table and then stood with his back arched, hissing at the corgis, who stood on their hind legs trying to reach him.

Some of the guests were taken by surprise and shrieked, while everyone who had been near the table jumped away.

'Treacle!' shouted Mr Pattacake, running towards him.

But Treacle completely ignored him, his mouth open and teeth bared in a hiss.

One of the footmen, who had been unpacking a hamper, grabbed the corgis' collars and dragged them away, while they struggled and yapped, trying to chase the cat who had dared to intrude into their territory.

'Down!' demanded Mr Pattacake, embarrassed again by Treacle's behaviour.

Treacle leapt down and scurried away. Mr Pattacake tried to straighten the tablecloth and put things back as they were, before the Queen came to greet her guests and noticed, although she would surely hear about the rumpus.

Mr Pattacake had almost recovered from the humiliation when one of the security men came up to him.

'There is a family outside who says it was *their* picnic you had prepared. They followed the balloon when it took off, and are now waiting outside the front gates of the palace.'

'Oh dear,' said Mr Pattacake nervously as he suddenly remembered. 'Mr & Mrs Martin and their children, Oliver and Sally.'

'That is the name they gave,' said the footman, nodding. 'This is a very strange situation indeed and I shall have to see what we can do.'

A few minutes later, Mr Pattacake saw the family arrive, looking round them in awe. The children spotted Mr Pattacake and ran up to him, smiling.

'Wow! Mr Pattacake,' said Oliver. 'You landed *here*!'

'And the Queen said that as we missed our balloon flight, we could join the garden party,' said Sally happily. The children jumped up and down with excitement.

Their parents walked up to join them.

'I can't believe this, Mr Pattacake,' said Mrs Martin. 'What a wonderful birthday present!'

'It was accidental,' said Mr Pattacake, chuckling. 'I really didn't mean to land here.'

They all went into a marquee and helped themselves to the food. Mr Pattacake was delighted to see how popular his own food was, especially the chocolate mice. He doubted that chocolate mice had even been served at a royal garden party before.

The Queen came out and mingled with the crowd. She made a special point of greeting the Martin family, and nodded again to Mr Pattacake. No mention was made of the corgis and Treacle, thankfully.

But where *was* that cat?

The Martins had offered to take Mr Pattacake and Treacle back to the balloon launch site where he had left his little yellow van. They certainly couldn't go back the way they had come! Mr Pattacake went to look for Treacle.

He was nowhere near the balloon basket, or anywhere else in sight. Could he have actually gone into the palace? Mr Pattacake certainly hoped not.

Finally, he found Treacle up one of the trees by the lake.

'I do believe you're afraid of those corgis!' teased Mr Pattacake.

Treacle looked down at him, scowling.

'Oh, I know, it was three against one.' Mr
Pattacake said, smiling. 'Come on everyone, it's
time to go home.'

There were, however, two more surprises before the adventure was over.

One of the Queen's corgis had just had puppies, and the Queen gave one to the Martin family as a reminder of their surprise visit to the palace – as if anyone was likely to forget.

The second surprise came about a week later. Another letter with the Queen's crest on the envelope was dropped through Mr Pattacake's letterbox.

'How exciting!' exclaimed Mr Pattacake. He opened it up and read it out to Treacle.

'Dear Mr Pattacake,

Her Majesty, the Queen, thanks you for
providing the excellent extra food for the garden
party. The chocolate mice were especially popular
with her great-grandchildren and she would like to
place a permanent order for a box of twenty each
month.

With good wishes,

John Dearman, Equerry to the Queen.'

Mr Pattacake looked up. 'We have a royal commission, Treacle!' he said as his new big chef's hat wobbled with excitement. But Treacle just curled up in a ball and closed his eyes.